To All Those Beautiful I's Out There Especially
Martha, Frank, Mark, Calvin, Kaitlin, and Lauren!
~KSS

For Ken, Jordan and Brenden, with love
~JKS

Published by
Book Publishers Network
P.O. Box 2256
Bothell, WA 98041
(425) 483-3040

ISBN 0-9755407-1-8
Library of Congress Number: 2004110886

Printed in Korea
10 9 8 7 6 5 4 3 2

Book Design by Joyce Sandness

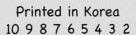
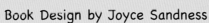

GLASSES,

GLASSES

OH WHAT DO I SEE?

Story and Illustrations by
Karen Smith Stair

Graphic Design by
Joyce Sandness

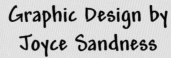

When I was oh so little
about the age of three,
all I could see was
Blurries and Squiggles,
and that is how I thought
it was supposed to be.

Everyone said,
"What big beautiful eyes he has!"
But they didn't know
and I couldn't say,
that these big beautiful eyes
didn't see the right way!

I was starting to squint
to make everything more clear.
The Blurries and Squiggles
were not going away
and I was starting to fear.

So, mom took me to the "I"
doctor to get my I's tested.
To pass time, we played with
toys, blocks, puzzles,
and even rested!

The doctor had me look at a
big chart, then put some drops
in my eyes. Next, she put
funny glasses on me
that made me look like a fly.
We were laughing quite a bit,
my mom and I!

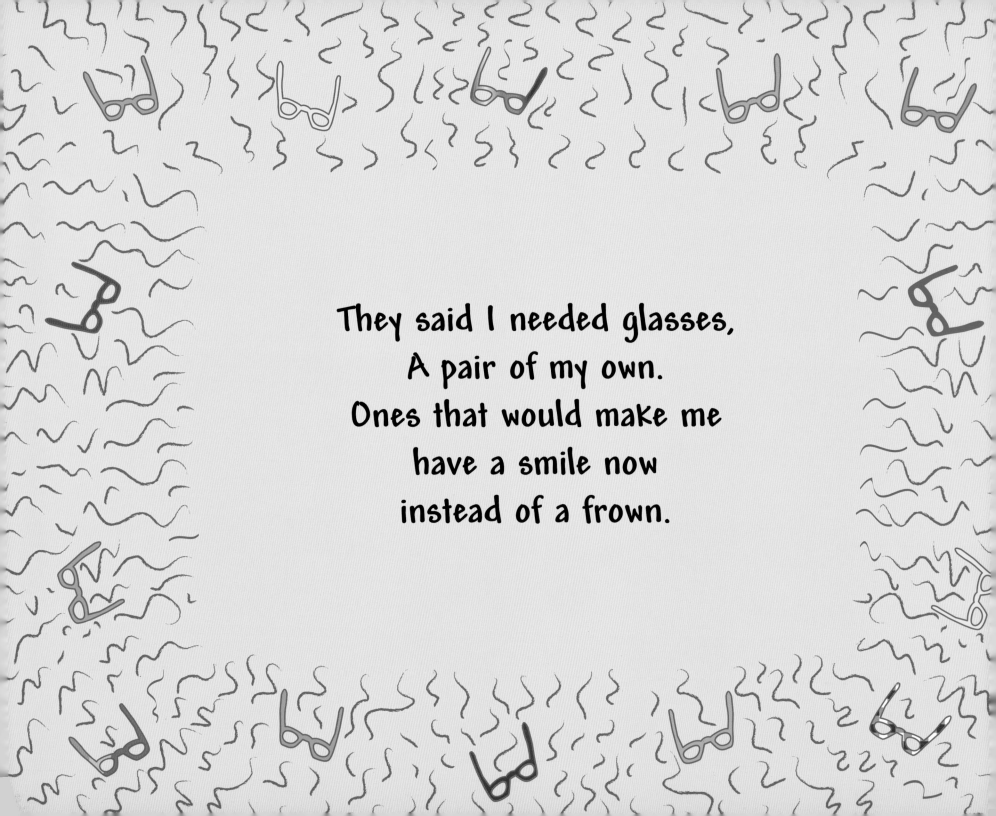

They said I needed glasses,
A pair of my own.
Ones that would make me
have a smile now
instead of a frown.

But choose which ones?
Do I get just one pair?
Blue, green, red or yellow,
Should they match my hair?

The I doctor called
My new glasses were here!
I was so excited
I started to cheer!
We went back to the I Doctor
to try on my new gear.

I put them on and,
OH MY, EVERYTHING
WAS SO CLEAR!
It brought such a smile to
my face, I was grinning
from ear to ear!

The first thing I saw with my
brand new clear sight,
was the smile on my mom
who said everything now
will be all right.

She had something else
besides that smile
that I saw very clear.
On her cheek,
all shiny and bright,
was a tear.

My mom says she will
never forget that day.
For that smile on MY face,
she says,
is in her heart to stay!

GLASSES, GLASSES
OH WHAT DO I SEE?

I CAN FINALLY SEE
THE MOST BEAUTIFUL ME!!

I
LOVE
MY NEW GLA
SSES I LOOKS
O CUTE AND SO DO
you!

Sight. What a wonderful, joyous thing it is to be able to see and see clearly, to see flower fields in the distance or the face of a loved one up close. Our first child could not see clearly and we did not know. How could he tell us everything was blurry when that is all he knew? This is our story. When Calvin was about three years old, I noticed his left eye turned inward for a second while looking at me from across the room. I did not think anything of it until a week or so later when it happened again. I said something is not quite right! We made an appointment to see an "I" Doctor. Calvin was diagnosed as farsighted with strabismus. His left eye was weaker than his right eye but both farsighted. Normal vision is where light enters the eye and directly focuses on the retina. Farsighted is where light enters the eye but focuses behind the retina. Nearsighted is where light enters the eye but focuses in front of the retina. With Calvin's new glasses he had to wear a patch over his right eye for a few months until his left eye was strengthened. We were told that it was very important to treat the strabismus or Calvin's binocular vision would not develop correctly. We are So glad for all of the wonderful "I" Doctors out there! On the next few pages there is information on doctors, statistics, and websites. I do not endorse any of these websites. They are listed as helpful resources for your children's I health. We hope you learn something from our story and get your boys and girls beautiful "I"s checked. HAPPY "I"s TO ALL!

The Three O's: Information from The EyeCare Connection (www.eyecarecontacts.com)

The OPTOMETRIST is a Doctor of Optometry (O.D.) and a primary vision care specialist having completed four years of college and a four year doctoral program. The O.D. can examine eyes for health and vision disorders, treat with corrective lenses and exercises, and may also treat certain eye diseases.

The OPHTHALMOLOGIST is a Doctor of Ophthalmology (M.D.) and a primary and secondary medical/surgical eye care provider having completed four years of college, four years of medical school, and at least two years of residency relating to the diagnosis and treatment, including surgery, of diseases of the eye.

The OPTICIAN is a person trained in the skills necessary to grind and shape materials to the optical powers as prescribed by an O.D. or M.D. Education consists of trade school with certification. In the U.S., they can not examine eyes.

-Twenty-five percent of children ages 5-12 have a vision problem that could affect their educational performance, yet only fourteen percent of pre-school aged children and only thirty-one percent of children ages 6-16 have had any comprehensive eye exams (Managed Healthcare, "Vision Screening for Children" 7/99)
National Center for Health Statistics

-Vision disorders are the fourth most common disability in the U.S. and the most prevalent handicapping condition in childhood. Between 8-12 million children are affected.
American Foundation for Vision Awareness

<u>Websites</u>

American Academy of Ophthalmology: www.aao.org

The American Association for Pediatric Ophthalmology and
      Strabismus(AAPOS): www.aapos.org

College of Optometrists in Vision Development: www.covd.org

Optometric Extension Program: www.oep.org

Parents Active for Vision Education: www.pavevision.org

Special thanks to Mary E. Baker, O.D., Optometric Physician for her valuable time and information.

CHILD'S HEALTH INFORMATION

Child's Name: _____

Pediatrician Name & Phone: _____

Checkups: _____

1 Doctor Name & Phone: _____

Newborn to 3 months: _____

6 months to 1 year: _____

3 years (approximate): _____

5 years (approximate): _____

Check-Ups: Opthalmologists recommend the above schedule for pediatric exams by trained Opthalmologists or Pediatricians*   (*AAO.org)

Notes:

_____

_____

_____

_____

_____

_____

_____

_____

_____

_____

_____